Mermaids
in the
Backyard

Mermaids
in the
Backyard

by Catherine Hapka

illustrated by Patricia Castelao

A STEPPING STONE BOOK™

Random House 🏠 New York

Text copyright © 2013 by Catherine Hapka
Cover art and interior illustrations copyright © 2013 by Patricia Castelao

All rights reserved. Published in the United States by Random House Children's Books, a division of Random House, Inc., New York.

Random House and the colophon are registered trademarks and A Stepping Stone Book and the colophon are trademarks of Random House, Inc.

Visit us on the Web!
SteppingStonesBooks.com
randomhouse.com/kids

Educators and librarians, for a variety of teaching tools, visit us at
RHTeachersLibrarians.com

Library of Congress Cataloging-in-Publication Data
Hapka, Cathy.
Mermaids in the backyard / Catherine Hapka ; illustrated by Patricia Castelao. — 1st ed.
p. cm. — (A Stepping Stone Book)
Summary: When her family moves from Chicago to an island in South Carolina,
Lindy is sure she will be unhappy until she makes a surprising
discovery in the backyard of their beach house.
ISBN 978-0-307-97637-6 (trade) — ISBN 978-0-375-97120-4 (lib. bdg.) —
ISBN 978-0-307-97638-3 (ebook)
[1. Mermaids—Fiction. 2. Ocean—Fiction. 3. Moving, Household—Fiction.]
I. Castelao, Patricia, ill. II. Title.
PZ7.H1996Mer 2013   [E]—dc23   2012002297

Printed in the United States of America

10 9 8 7 6 5 4 3 2 1

Random House Children's Books supports the First Amendment
and celebrates the right to read.

Contents

Prologue

"What should we do today?" Coral asked her sister, Sealily.

It was a peaceful morning under the sea. The sisters were floating out of their family's cave with their pet sea horse, Finneus. Bright sunlight shone all the way to the seafloor from far overhead. The light made the water sparkle. It brought out coppery glints in Coral's hair and silvery ones in Sealily's.

"Let's go look for sea stars in the shallows," Sealily said with a swish of her tail. Her lavender and green scales glittered like jewels.

Coral shook her head. "You know we're not allowed to go to the shallows. Besides,

1

Pelagos says there's going to be a storm soon. Let's find some dolphins instead."

Sealily floated in place and thought about that. She loved grabbing a ride on a friendly dolphin.

But they had gone dolphin riding three days ago. Sealily wanted to do something different. She loved swimming when fierce storms raged overhead in the Drylands. Most of all, she loved surfing the wind-whipped water along the surface.

She knew she'd get in big trouble if her parents ever found out. Merpeople weren't supposed to go above the surface. Never, ever. It was the strictest rule under the sea.

But Sealily couldn't resist, no matter how much Coral scolded. Coral was much more careful than Sealily. Yet she never tattled on her. Never, ever. Sealily was happy that Coral was her big sister.

"Okay," she said. "We can go dolphin riding today."

"Good." Coral looked relieved.

Sealily smiled. "But tomorrow we're going to the shallows," she added. "Whether grumpy old Pelagos likes it or not."

"We'll see." Coral shot upward. A school of minnows parted to let her pass, bubbling busily. Finneus squeaked and darted after her.

Yes, Coral could be way too careful. But she was crazy about anything to do with Drylanders. Sealily knew they would be heading toward the shore tomorrow, no matter what worries Coral might have about breaking the rules.

"Race you to the kelp forest," Sealily cried. Flicking her tail, she zipped after her sister.

The Bug House

"No way," Lindy Michaels said, staring through the car window. "We're going to live *here*?"

"Isn't it adorable?" her mom said.

Lindy didn't know what to say. The house looked like a giant bug. It was tall and narrow and stood on stilts. She could see right underneath it to the ocean. There were three floors above the stilts. The first two floors each had a white slatted porch sticking out at a different angle. Windows of every shape and size stared in all directions. Grayish-blue shingles covered everything in between.

Even the yard was weird. It was June, but there was no normal green grass in sight— just tall yellowish grass that waved in the sea breeze and looked as if it would cut Lindy's hand if she touched it. And lots of rocks and sand and scrubby-looking palms.

Behind the crazy stilt-bug house, the ground sloped down to the water's edge. A huge tree with wide, spreading branches stood at the front corner of the house. It looked as if the tree was trying to push the whole house down the hill into the sea.

Lindy's father steered the car into the driveway. At least Lindy guessed it was a driveway. It wasn't anything like their drive-way in Chicago. That one was paved and smooth, with tidy shrubs lining both sides.

This one was made of bumpy gravel and

broken seashells. It curved sharply to go around a big clump of boulders. Finally Mr. Michaels stopped the car.

"Come on, dear," Lindy's mom said. "We'll show you your room."

Lindy climbed out of the car as slowly as she could. Whatever room they were about to show her, it wasn't *her* room. *Her* room was back home in Chicago. The only room she'd known for her entire nine years of life.

Her parents had always talked about leaving the city and their office jobs someday. They wanted to live on the beach and run a nice little tourist business. They'd planned to wait until after Lindy went away to college.

Then Lindy's aunt had vacationed in South Carolina and noticed a boat business for sale. Lindy's parents had decided it was fate. It was time to follow their dreams—now.

Lindy tugged on a strand of her dark hair. Her best friend, Tara, liked to tease her about that habit. She said Lindy would pull out all her hair and end up as bald as Mr. Dann, their third-grade math teacher.

Thinking about Tara—and even about Mr. Dann—made Lindy sad. What was Tara doing right now? Was she wearing the bracelet Lindy had made her as a good-bye present?

Lindy reached into the car and grabbed her pink backpack. Her going-away gift from Tara was inside. Lindy wanted to unzip the flap so she could touch it. But she didn't want her parents to see.

"Your room is on the top floor," Lindy's mom said. "Isn't that cool? You'll be able to see the whole island."

"And the ocean," Mr. Michaels said with a wink. "You can watch for sea monsters and pirate ships from up there."

Usually Lindy loved her dad's goofy sense of humor. He could almost always make her laugh.

She wasn't in the mood to laugh right now, though. She felt more like crying. She blinked her eyes very fast to stop the tears from coming. When she looked at her parents to see if they'd noticed, they were staring in the other direction.

"Well, hello there!" her father called out cheerfully. Mrs. Michaels waved and smiled.

They were looking toward the left side of the house. It was very rocky over there. Stones of all shapes and sizes covered a steep slope, down from the sandy side yard. At the bottom, a row of craggy gray boulders stood at the edge of the water, holding back the waves. The boulders looked like a line of hunched-over old men. There was even bright green moss on some that looked like hair.

A boy around Lindy's age was on the near side of the boulders. He was standing in a large puddle in the rocky ground. Scrambling out of the water, he sloshed along a narrow, sandy path up the hill. The path led toward Lindy and her parents.

Lindy watched the boy. He had messy brown hair that looked like it should have a bird nesting in it. His shoulders were sunburned, and he wore faded board shorts and flip-flops. Dangling from one hand was a slimy-looking orange starfish.

"Hi," he said when he reached them. "Are you the new people on the island?"

"Yes, we are," Lindy's mom said. "We're the Michaels family. We're moving in today."

"I'm Matthew. I live over there." Matthew waved the starfish toward some scrubby trees to the right of the bug house.

"Matthew!" a new voice called. "Where are you?"

A girl hurried into sight between the trees. She was about twelve years old and had light brown hair with sunny blond streaks. She was carrying a baby dressed in a sparkly green bathing suit with a mermaid's tail.

Matthew made a face and pointed at the baby. "That's one of my little sisters," he said.

"There you are!" the older girl said when she saw him. "I thought you were going to help me watch the babies so they could play in the water." Then she noticed the others. "Oh! Hello. You must be the Michaels family."

"That's right," Lindy's dad said with a smile. "Are you Matthew's sister?"

"No way!" Matthew said quickly. "She's Jessica. She lives down the road."

12

Jessica laughed. "I'm Jessica Trenton. Welcome to Little Hermit's Cove."

"Thank you, Jessica. It's lovely to meet you," Lindy's mom said. "And you and your sister, too, Matthew."

"He has two more little sisters. They're triplets." Jessica shifted the baby she was holding to her other hip. "Isn't that cool?"

Matthew rolled his eyes. "Only if you don't have to smell their stinky diapers," he said.

"Gross," Lindy muttered. Her parents chuckled.

"This is our daughter," Mr. Michaels said. "Lindy, say hello to Jessica and Matthew."

Lindy guessed that someone Jessica's age probably didn't care about meeting someone her age. And she could already tell Matthew was the kind of boy she wouldn't like.

Loud, messy, and annoying.

Jessica gave her a friendly smile. "Hi, Lindy," she said. "You're going to love living here. Little Hermit's Island is the coolest place in the world."

"Hi." Lindy couldn't think of anything else to say. Sure, the island seemed kind of cool. It would be a nice place to visit on vacation. But how would she ever get used to *living* there?

Sharks and Sparks

"This is it." Mr. Michaels spread out his arms and turned in a circle. He had a big smile on his face. "Our new office! Isn't it great?"

The Michaels family, Jessica, and Matthew were standing on a wooden pier. Small waves lapped against the pillars. Boats tied to the pier bumped gently against one another as the water rocked them back and forth. Overhead, seagulls circled and swooped, letting out a chorus of noisy cries. Everything smelled like salt and seaweed. At least Lindy guessed it was seaweed.

"What do you think, Lindy?" Mrs. Michaels asked. "With a little luck, your father and I will turn this place into the best boat dock in South Carolina!"

"The dock used to be really popular with tourists," Jessica said. "Then Mr. Lewis got sick and moved to the mainland. Nobody wanted to take it over until you guys bought it."

Jessica had left the mermaid-suited baby

with Matthew's dad so she could show Mr. and Mrs. Michaels a shortcut from the bug house to the dock. Matthew had tossed his starfish back in the water and tagged along.

The boat dock was about a quarter of a mile from the house. They could walk there on the road, or they could take Jessica's shortcut, a twisty, sandy path along the edge of the cove.

Now here they were. Lindy looked around. The sun was so bright she had to squint. The dock was right in the middle of the cove, a blobby inlet cutting into one end of the island. Houses lined the shore of the cove. A cluster of shops and restaurants stood just south of the dock. People strolled around looking sunburned and happy. More people were swimming in the shallows off a narrow strip of pale sand. Half a dozen boats floated on the sparkling, sunlit water. One was a big sailboat heading toward the open sea beyond the cove, and another was a rowboat with a pair of kids rowing it.

"Hey! Earth to New Girl."

Lindy blinked. Matthew was waving his hand in front of her face. There was dirt under his fingernails and a grubby Band-Aid on one thumb. It looked like it had been there for at least a month.

Lindy's parents were walking farther down the pier, checking out the boats. She hoped they wouldn't fall in. "Are there sharks out there?" she asked.

Jessica smiled. "Don't worry. Sharks hardly ever come into the cove. At least not the big ones."

"You'll probably see some by your house, though," Matthew said. "You're right at the mouth of the cove. There are tons of sharks out on the ocean side." He smirked. "So don't go swimming alone, or you might come back with one leg missing."

"That's not funny!" Lindy shivered.

"He's just trying to scare you," Jessica said in a soothing voice. "Still, you probably shouldn't swim in the ocean. Not until you get used to being near the water, anyway."

"I *am* used to being near the water," Lindy said. "Chicago is right on Lake Michigan. That's a huge lake. Like, *really* huge."

Jessica didn't look very impressed. "Okay. But the ocean is different. You'll see once you've been here awhile."

Lindy didn't answer. Instead, she walked a little farther out on the pier.

"Ow!" she cried as her toe caught on a loose board. She stumbled forward. When she put out her hands to catch herself, she realized she was falling straight toward the water! Just in time, she staggered sideways onto her other foot.

"Are you okay?" Jessica asked.

Matthew laughed. "If you want to go swimming, just say so!"

"Shut up." Lindy scowled at him. She was sensitive about being clumsy. Even Tara

would never tease her about it.

Then she stared out at the water. The waves seemed to dance, throwing sparks from the sun. It was hard to see clearly. But Lindy thought she spotted something near the mouth of the cove. Was it—could it be a person's head popping up from the water?

She squinted, taking a step forward.

"Careful," Matthew said. "You don't want to fall in for real this time. The sharks might get you."

Lindy ignored him. "Do you see that?"

"See what?" Jessica asked.

"It looks like somebody's out there! Right by those big rocks and trees and stuff."

"That's where your house is," Matthew said. "If the trees weren't there, you could see it from here."

Lindy glanced over at the shore. Sure enough, the shrubby trees looked familiar. When she looked back out at the water, there was no sign of anything other than waves.

"Oh," she said. "They're gone. What if it was somebody drowning? Shouldn't we tell someone?" She looked toward the lifeguard chair on the beach.

Jessica chuckled. "I'm sure there's no one there. Just your eyes playing tricks on you because of the bright sun shining on the water."

Before Lindy could answer, her parents came walking back. They looked happy and excited. Her mother's hair had mostly escaped from its bun and was blowing around in the breeze. Her father's feet were hairy and ghostly pale in his brand-new sandals.

"Well, kids?" Mr. Michaels said. "Want to take one of these babies out for a spin?" He waved toward the boats tied to the pier.

"Sure!" Matthew said. "We have our own motorboat. So I can totally show you how to drive one."

Jessica checked her watch. "I'll come, too, thanks. Can you please drop me off at

Matthew's house? They have a dock."

"Absolutely." Mr. Michaels beamed. "Come on, Lindy. All aboard!"

Lindy smiled weakly. Her parents seemed really excited to start their new life in Little Hermit's Cove. But she was afraid that she'd never, ever fit in.

3

A Stormy Surprise

Lindy stared out the living room window. Rain ran rivers down the panes. Out on the ocean, the waves seemed confused. Instead of lapping gently and evenly against the shore, they crashed against one another, sending white spray everywhere. Watching them made Lindy nervous.

She looked down at the old-man boulders. The ocean was already halfway up their backs. Every few seconds a wave crashed against them. Each time, more water flowed over the tops of the boulders. Some of it splashed into the tide pool where Matthew had found that starfish the day before. The rest splattered onto the rocky ground or got mixed up with the rain.

Lightning cracked the sky in two. Thunder snarled like a giant, belching monster. The sound made the whole house shake. Lindy wished her parents would hurry home. It was too stormy to go to the dock that day, so they'd taken the ferry to the mainland to shop for supplies.

An even bigger crash of thunder rattled the windows. A second later the phone rang, making Lindy jump. She hurried to answer it.

"Hello, Lindy?" Her mother's voice sounded crackly and far away. "Can you hear me?"

"Where are you?" Lindy asked. "Are you going to be home soon?"

"I'm afraid not." The phone crackled again, making it impossible for Lindy to hear the next few words. Then it cut back in. ". . . and they said it's not safe to take the ferry out until the storm passes. So we're stuck on the mainland for a while."

"What?" Lindy tightened her grip on the phone.

"Don't worry—your father is on his cell right now talking to Jessica. She's going to run over and sit with you."

"She doesn't have to do that," Lindy said quickly. She hated the idea of staying alone in the creaking, swaying house. But she hated the thought of needing a babysitter even more.

Once again, a crackle of static swallowed her mother's voice. ". . . but she'll be there as soon as she can."

"Mom?" Lindy said as her mother's voice cut out. "Hello?"

The phone was dead. Lindy set it down and tugged at her hair. Now what? Suddenly she hoped Jessica would get there quickly.

She looked out the back window. In the wind and rain, the yard looked like it belonged on some distant, sandy planet. The wind kept blowing the branches of the big tree against the side of the house. It sounded as if it was knocking to come inside.

The ocean looked more frantic than ever. Lindy hoped the waves wouldn't grab the bug house and pull it right into the sea. She shivered at the thought. Maybe it would float off like the houseboat she'd once seen on TV. Her room on the top floor would stick up like a buoy, swaying with the current.

Then again, maybe the house would sink

to the bottom of the ocean. Fish would swim in through all the windows, and barnacles would attach themselves everywhere. Maybe one would even stick to her dad's bald spot when he came home.

The thought made her smile a little. She stared out to sea, wondering if it was as stormy beneath the waves as it was on the surface. Were the fish waiting for the storm to pass just like she was?

Her gaze slid closer to shore. The water was still rising behind the line of old-man boulders at the bottom of the hill. The huge rocks seemed to hunker down as waves kept crashing against them, sending more spray flying everywhere.

Then she saw something else. She leaned closer to the window. It was hard to see through the blowing rain. Was there really something moving out there by the old men?

Maybe it's Jessica, she thought.

Resting both hands on the glass, Lindy pressed her face to the window. There! She saw movement again. It looked as if some-one was sitting in the tide pool.

"Matthew wouldn't be crazy enough to poke around out there *now,* would he?" Lindy mumbled. She squinted harder, trying to see past the streams running down the window.

Thinking about Matthew reminded her of the day before. He and Jessica hadn't believed that Lindy had seen someone out in the cove. Could they have been right? Had her eyes been playing tricks on her?

The wind blew the rain away from the window for a second, giving her a better look at the tide pool. She gasped. She wasn't

seeing things. There was a person out there!

"Help!" The storm was so loud that Lindy could barely hear the cry, even though the windows were cracked open to keep the house from getting too stuffy.

Her arms and legs started to tremble. Who was out there?

She raced to the front window and looked out. Still no sign of Jessica.

The cry came again. This time it was drowned out by another rumble of thunder.

Lindy clenched her fists to stop her hands from shaking. She'd never been so scared in her life. Yet she knew she had to try to help the person out there.

The wind grabbed Lindy as she dove out the front door. She held tightly to the handrail, worried that she might fall down the wet wooden steps. Somehow she made it safely to the bottom. She had to lean forward to make any headway against the wind-lashed rain.

It seemed to take forever to reach the rocky side yard. As soon as she did, Lindy knew she hadn't been seeing things. There was a girl in the tide pool by the old-man rocks! She had long silvery-blond hair plastered to her head by the rain. Her soggy green top clung to her pale torso.

"Hey!" Lindy called. She skidded down the slope on the sandy path. "Are you okay?"

The girl turned to look at her. Her eyes were huge and frightened. She cried out, but the wind swept the words away before Lindy could hear them.

Lindy's heart pounded as she fought the wind and the rain-slick rocks to get closer to the tide pool. She felt like she did in scary

dreams sometimes, when she ran and ran and couldn't get anywhere.

Just then she heard another cry for help. This time it wasn't coming from the girl in the tide pool.

Glancing at the old-man rocks, Lindy saw another girl peering over one of them. She had coppery-blond hair and aqua eyes.

"Please help my sister!" she cried, clinging to the wet boulder with both arms. "She
thought she could surf the storm. Now she's
stuck!"

The second girl seemed to be around
Lindy's age, and the first maybe a year
younger. Why were they allowed to surf
in such a terrible storm? And why was the

younger sister stuck? Lindy had seen Matthew wading in that tide pool yesterday. Even with the extra water from the storm, it couldn't be more than two feet deep. Was the girl hurt?

The waves rolled out. Some of the water drew back out of the pool, swirling around the boulders. Lindy's eyes widened as she got a better look at the blond girl.

Instead of legs, she had a long tail covered in shiny green scales tinted with lavender. A pair of lavender tail fins flapped helplessly in the air.

The girl in the tide pool was a mermaid!

Mermaids Are Real!

"No way!" Lindy blurted out. "There's no such thing as mermaids!"

"Please!" The girl in the tide pool sounded terrified. "I have to get back to the sea!"

"Can you help us?" the older girl asked, still clinging to the rock.

When Lindy looked at her, she could see the tip of a tail swing up as the waves rolled in again. The older girl was a mermaid, too!

Lindy's mind swirled with questions. But one thing was clear. These girls—these

37

mermaids—were in trouble. She had to help them.

"What's the matter?" Lindy asked the younger sister. "Can't you get back to the ocean?"

"I've been trying and trying!" the mermaid answered, the words pouring out of her. "The waves swept over those rocks and trapped me here in the shallows!"

Lindy looked around and saw what she meant. The water came at least halfway up the old-man rocks on the ocean side. On this side, though, the boulders rose as high as her head. The mermaid would have to go all the way up the hill to get around them.

"I told you we shouldn't come so close, Sealily," the older mermaid said.

Lindy blinked away the rain running into her eyes. "Sealily?" She looked at the younger of the two girls. "Is that your name?"

Sealily nodded. "Yes. That's my sister, Coral."

Lindy glanced at the other mermaid, who smiled uncertainly. Just then the wind shifted and the rain lightened. In that moment, Lindy was able to look clearly into Coral's face. Suddenly she had the strangest feeling

that, somehow, she already knew her. That the two of them were meant to be friends. Maybe *best* friends. It was the strangest—and nicest—feeling Lindy had ever had outside of a dream.

"Nice to meet you," she said, feeling shy as she smiled back. "I'm Lindy."

"Lindy—that's a funny name." Sealily's voice sounded faint. A second later she fell facedown into the water of the tide pool.

That made Lindy forget all about strange feelings and everything else. "Oh no! Did she faint?"

"No, she's okay," Coral said. "Merpeople can't breathe for long without water. That's why Sealily can't stay there in the shallows. Or Finneus, either." Worry crept back into her voice.

"Finneus?" Lindy said.

Sealily sat up just in time to hear her. "Come say hi to Lindy, Finny," she called in a singsong voice. "She's the Drylander who's going to save us!"

For a second nothing happened. Then a small yellow creature popped into view beside Sealily. It had a knobby head that looked like it belonged to a cute little dragon.

"Oh! A sea horse!" Lindy exclaimed.

The sea horse let out a squeak of alarm and ducked beneath the surface again. "That's Finneus," Sealily told Lindy. "He's shy with strangers."

"He's our pet," Coral added. "He follows us everywhere."

Part of Lindy's brain was still struggling with the whole idea of mermaids, never mind pet sea horses. But another part was figuring out the problem.

"So the waves tossed you in here," she said, pointing at the pool. "Then the big rocks kept you from swimming back out."

"Yes," Sealily said. "And the small rocks, too. When I tried to crawl over them, they hurt my tail."

Lindy looked at the hilly ground around the tide pool. Sharp rocks were scattered everywhere. Well, *almost* everywhere.

"What about going that way?" She pointed back the way she'd come. There was a short rocky area at the edge of the pool in that direction. Beyond was the soft sand of the path leading up toward the house.

Coral looked worried. "She can't breathe out of the water long enough to crawl all the way around. We're too slow on the Drylands." She flicked the end of her tail for emphasis, then disappeared.

Lindy guessed she was diving back down into the water to breathe. Sure enough, the mergirl returned with the next wave.

"I have an idea," Lindy told Coral and Sealily. "I'll be right back."

She raced away. Several times she almost tripped or slipped. Finally she reached the open area beneath the bug house. It was nice to be out of the driving rain, though the wind still blew salt spray in.

Dodging through the maze of stilts, Lindy made her way to the huge concrete beam at the center. There, on a row of hooks, hung several bright orange life jackets. She slung one over her arm, then ran back out into the storm. Soon she was back at the tide pool.

"What's that?" Sealily asked.

"You can lie on this," Lindy explained. "I'll pull the straps and drag you. That way the rocks won't cut you on the way to the path. And I can pull you around on the sand faster than you could crawl."

Coral stared at Lindy, her eyes huge with worry. "Are you sure you can pull her fast enough? She'll only have a few minutes."

"Of course!" But suddenly Lindy *wasn't* sure. "Uh, or if you want, we could wait for Jessica to get here. Then she can help."

Coral looked even more alarmed. "No!" she cried. "No one else can see us! We're in enough trouble already, letting one Dry-lander see us! If our people find out . . ."

"Okay, okay," Lindy said. "Don't worry. I'm sure I can do it myself."

"Good," Sealily said. "Come on, Finny. Let's get you out of here first. Go with Coral." She scooped up the little sea horse. He immediately wriggled free and popped back into the water, chirping loudly. Sealily grabbed him again. "Stop that," she scolded. "I'll be in the water with you soon."

Sealily stretched up, balancing on the last section of her tail. Coral stretched her arm out over the rocks as far as she could. She still couldn't quite reach Finneus.

"Maybe I can toss him over into the water," Sealily said.

"No!" Coral said. "The waves are too rough. He'd get smashed up against the rocks."

Lindy nodded. The sea horse *was* tiny— much smaller than Tara's pet Chihuahua. "Try handing him to me instead," she suggested. "I think I can reach Coral from here."

She reached toward Finneus. As soon as he saw her, the sea horse chirped loudly and tried to wriggle away. But Sealily held on to him.

"It's okay, Finny!" she said. "Lindy is our friend."

"That's right, Finneus," Lindy said softly. "I just want to help you."

Finneus stopped wriggling. He stared at Lindy with his tiny, dark eyes. When he chirped again, it sounded like a question.

"Good boy," Lindy cooed, slipping her

hands around Sealily's. Sealily slid hers out, leaving Lindy holding Finneus. His skin felt cool and lumpy.

Lindy stepped back, then stretched out with both hands. Coral was waiting, reaching over the rocks.

"I've got you, Finneus," Coral said as she grabbed him. She smiled at Lindy. "Thanks. I'll be right back."

"Finny likes you, Lindy Drylander," Sealily said as Coral disappeared with the sea horse. "He doesn't trust just anyone."

Lindy wasn't sure what to say. She'd never been trusted by a sea horse before. "I like him, too," she said.

Soon Coral reappeared on the other side of the old-man boulders. "Finneus is okay," she said. "Now it's your turn, Sealily. Are you sure you can do this?"

"I'm sure. Lindy Drylander will save me, just like she saved Finny. Let's go!" Sealily sounded almost cheerful. She stuck her face under the water for a second. Then she slithered out of the back of the pool and pulled herself onto the life jacket.

Lindy couldn't stop staring at her tail. Could this really be happening? Was she really helping to rescue a *mermaid*?

Sealily gripped the life jacket with both hands. "Ready!" she said.

"Hurry!" Coral urged. She turned and dove out of sight again.

Lindy grabbed the straps of the life jacket. She gave a tug, but nothing happened.

"Ready?" Sealily asked. Her voice already sounded breathier.

Lindy gulped. Should she just give up and wait for Jessica after all?

"Lindy! Are you coming?"

It was Coral. Lindy saw her bobbing in the surf just beyond the beach. It was hard to see through the rain, but Lindy thought she could make out Finneus's tiny yellow head beside her.

Seeing them made Lindy feel a little braver. She'd promised to help the sisters. She couldn't let them down just because she was scared.

She gave another pull on the straps. This time she felt the life jacket slide a little on the rocky ground. Another tug, and it slid even more.

Sealily hung on tight. She let out a cry that sounded like it might be a mermaid version of "Wheeeee!"

That made Lindy smile a little. She couldn't help noticing that Sealily's voice sounded weaker and shakier than ever, though. Pulling harder, she heard a *rrrrrip!* as the life jacket caught on a rock. Still, she kept pulling.

A few seconds later, the life jacket slipped onto the sand. Now all Lindy had to do was pull Sealily up the path and around the rocks. Then down the beach to the ocean.

Pull. Slide. Pull. Slide. Lindy's arms ached. But she kept going. Pull. Slide . . .

At last she crested the hill. She couldn't stop yet. Yanking the life jacket around the corner, she started pulling it down the beach. She expected it to be a lot easier now that they were going downhill instead of uphill. But the wet sand clung to the life jacket and slowed it down. When Lindy glanced back, Sealily looked pale. Her eyes were half closed, and she wasn't saying anything.

Pull. Slide. Pull. Slide. The water was only a few feet away. Lindy's muscles felt like jelly, and she could hear Sealily panting. Could they make it in time?

Then Lindy saw something else. Coral was crawling out of the surf. She looked scared but determined.

"We're coming!" Lindy called to her.

Pull. Slide. Pull. Slide.

Coral crawled forward and grabbed another strap. She pulled, wriggling backward toward the waves. Lindy glanced down at Coral's tail. It had to hurt her to crawl over the rough sand. Yet she wasn't complaining.

"Almost there," Lindy said, huffing and puffing.

"Ready," Sealily said faintly.

Lindy turned to look down at Sealily and saw the mermaid's eyes fluttering all the way shut. That gave Lindy extra strength. "Arrgh!" she cried, giving a big pull.

Her foot caught in the wet sand. She felt herself flying backward. But she kept hold of the straps. Her fall yanked the life jacket forward at the same moment an extra-large wave rolled onto the shore. It washed over Sealily, and she burst into motion. Both she and Coral spun through the water as gracefully as birds flitting through the air.

"Whew!" Lindy gasped. She hardly noticed when the wave poured over her. She was already soaked from the rain.

She rolled over to watch the mermaids swimming away. For a second she thought they weren't going to stop. But when the next wave rolled in, both sisters came with it. So did Finneus. He didn't seem shy at all now. Lindy laughed as the little sea horse bumped his head into her hand. He reminded her of her old neighbors' friendly Siamese cat.

"Thank you, Lindy Drylander!" Sealily cried joyfully, flicking her tail. "Thanks for helping us!"

"Yes." Coral wriggled closer and grasped Lindy by the hand. "We'll never forget you."

As the waves pulled out and the

mermaid's hand slipped out of hers, Lindy said, "I'll never forget you, either."

5

A Special Secret

"Hey!" someone cried.

Lindy spun around. Jessica was hurrying around the corner of the bug house. One hand clutched the hood of her raincoat to keep it from blowing off.

Oops. Lindy realized she'd been standing there staring out to sea ever since the mermaid sisters had disappeared beneath the waves.

"What are you doing out here?" Jessica demanded when she got closer. "Good thing I saw you before I called Sheriff Tom! I totally panicked when I got here and you weren't in the house. . . ."

There was more, but Lindy barely heard it. She still couldn't believe what had happened. Mermaids! She'd just met two real-life mermaids.

Finally Jessica noticed that she wasn't listening. "Are you okay?" she asked, looking worried. "What are you doing standing out here in the storm, anyway?"

"Nothing," Lindy said. "I guess I was just looking for, you know, sea monsters and, uh, mermaids." She held her breath. If Jessica had ever seen a mermaid around there, maybe she'd say so now.

Instead, Jessica just looked annoyed. "Stop goofing around. You could have been struck by lightning!"

Another yell came from up by the house.

Lindy looked over and saw Matthew jog-
ging toward them.

"What are you two doing out here?"
he asked.

"Getting wet," Jessica told him. "What about you?"

He grinned. "The triplets were screaming at all the thunder. I saw you guys over here, so I sneaked out."

Jessica rolled her eyes. "Come on," she ordered, sounding like a bossy babysitter. "Let's get inside before we all turn into fish!"

Or merpeople, Lindy thought, glancing out at the stormy sea. Then she turned and followed the others into the bug house.

That night Lindy dreamed about being a mermaid. In the dream, she lived with Coral and Sealily and Finneus in an undersea castle made of barnacles, coral, and life jackets. Whenever she wanted to go somewhere, she called a friendly whale. Once, the whale carried her all the way to Lake Michigan.

When they got there, Tara was waiting on the shore. She didn't believe in mermaids at first. But when she saw Lindy's shiny new tail, she laughed and laughed at the top of her lungs. . . .

Lindy woke up. Tara's laughter turned into a seagull's shrill cry. Several of the birds were calling loudly right outside her window.

Strong morning sunshine poured into Lindy's new room. The storm was finally over. The sky was an endless ceiling of blue except for a few high, fluffy clouds. Everything on the ground was still wet, though. Water droplets sparkled like jewels wherever Lindy looked.

All through breakfast, she couldn't stop thinking about the mermaid sisters. In the bright sunshine, even the storm seemed unreal. Could she have imagined the whole adventure?

Maybe I tripped and hit my head on a rock, she thought, stirring her cereal. The banana slices floating in it looked like little bald merpeople peeping up at her. *I heard people imagine weird stuff sometimes when they're unconscious.*

"Any plans today, Lindy?" her father asked, pouring himself more coffee. "Want to come help out at the dock?"

"What? Um, maybe." Lindy was too lost in thought to worry about her family's new business. "First I think I'll look around out-side. Okay?"

Her parents traded a glance. "All right," her mother said. "Why don't you put on your swimsuit? It's going to be a hot one out there today."

"If you're on the ocean side of the yard, don't wade out any deeper than your knees, okay, kiddo?" her father added. "I hear there's a wicked undertow just offshore."

"Don't worry." Lindy carried her bowl to the sink. "I'm not crazy enough to go swimming in the ocean. There could be sharks out there."

She went back to her room and put on her favorite pink and white swimsuit. Grabbing her backpack, she pulled out Tara's going-away gift. It was a Chicago Cubs T-shirt signed by several players. Lindy didn't care that much about sports, but Tara did. Lindy loved the T-shirt because it made her think of Tara.

Tara had warned her not to wear the shirt much so the autographs wouldn't fade. Lindy planned to ask her father to make a frame for it. She would hang it in her room to remind herself of Chicago.

"Maybe I'll wear it first, though," she whispered. "Just this once."

Soon Lindy was hurrying down the wooden steps wearing the Cubs T-shirt and a pair of shorts over her swimsuit. Her mother was right—it was hot. By the time she reached the bottom of the stairs, Lindy was already sweating.

She sat down on the beach just below the tide line. The waves were still rough and foamy after yesterday's storm. They splashed over her legs, cooling her off.

For a long time she just sat there looking at the ocean. Were there really merpeople out there? It was still pretty hard to believe, even though she'd seen them for herself.

Or at least she *thought* she had. . . .

After a while her parents came out. "We're heading over to the dock now," her dad said. "Sure you don't want to come?"

"No thanks," Lindy said. "I'm okay here."

Her mother looked worried. "You should get out and see more of the island, Lindy. That will help you settle in faster."

"It's not that," Lindy said. "It's too hot to walk that far, that's all."

Finally her parents left. As soon as they were out of sight, Lindy felt lonely. This place was too empty. Too quiet.

Well, maybe not exactly *quiet*. There was the constant pounding and sighing of the sea, plus the cries of seagulls overhead.

Then she heard a different sound: "Lindy!"

Lindy gasped. Bobbing just beyond the

surf were two heads. One had bright silvery-blond hair. The other had hair of coppery ginger.

It was the mermaids!

6

Good-bye for Good?

Lindy waded out as far as she dared. The busy waves grabbed at her legs, soaking the hem of her shorts.

Coral and Sealily waved, then dove beneath the surface. Seconds later they appeared closer to shore. The waves picked them up and carried them along.

"You came back!" Lindy cried when they reached her. "Hi, Finneus," she added when the sea horse popped into view.

Finneus chirped and bumped at her leg with his head. Lindy smiled and patted him.

Sealily laughed. It sounded like water trickling over bells. "We came to thank you again, Lindy the hero."

"Yes." Coral glanced around nervously. "But we can't stay long. It's not safe for us to be so close to the Drylands."

"I still can't believe you guys are real." Lindy stared at the mermaids' graceful, shimmering tails. "I didn't believe there were really mermaids."

"We weren't sure what Drylanders would be like," Coral said. "We never know whether to believe the stories Pelagos tells us."

An extra-rough wave rushed past, shoving at Lindy's legs so fiercely that it almost knocked her down. For a second Lindy panicked. What if she lost her balance and the waves pulled her out to sea?

Then she remembered: Her new friends

were there. They wouldn't let her get washed away.

"Who's Pelagos?" she asked them.

"He lives in the next cave with his mer-lady, Thetis. They taught us everything we know about Drylanders," Sealily said.

"Oh! That reminds me," Coral said. "Thetis told me something once. I've always wondered if it was true. Wait here—I'll be right back."

She turned and swam back out to sea, her coppery hair streaming behind her. With a flip of her tail, she disappeared into the depths.

"Where'd she go?" Lindy asked.

Sealily shrugged. "I don't know. Here, watch this—I've been teaching Finny a new trick."

For the next few minutes, she tried to

get Finneus to do a flip by swirling her hand around in the water. Finneus watched her but stayed right where he was. When Sealily tried to turn him over to show him what she meant, he spit water into her face and darted away.

Lindy laughed. "I guess Finny doesn't want to do tricks."

Finally Coral returned, breathless and excited. "I found it!" she cried. Clutched in her hand was a pair of tiny white blobs.

"What's that?" Lindy asked.

"Thetis told me that in long-ago days, Drylanders used a special type of sea sponge to breathe underwater," Coral explained. "That's one reason Sealily and I first came to this spot. Thetis says it's one of the only places these sponges are found."

"It is?" Sealily cried. "You didn't tell me that, Coral!"

Coral looked sheepish. "I wasn't sure it was true."

Sealily giggled. "Right. Thetis doesn't know everything she thinks she knows." She spun in the water to face Lindy, her eyes sparkling. "You have to see if it works, Lindy Drylander!"

Coral held out the sponges. "If you plug your nose with them, you should be able to breathe just like a mermaid," she told Lindy. "Then we can show you our world!"

Swimming around under the sea had been fun in Lindy's dream. The thought of doing it for real was pretty scary, though. The idea of sticking those slimy little things in her nose wasn't much better.

"I wish I could," she said. "But I'm not a very good swimmer."

"We'll help you," Sealily urged. "Please,

will you try it, Lindy Drylander?"

Just then another big wave rushed in. Finneus squeaked as it grabbed him. Sealily reached out and caught him before the wave could carry him all the way to shore. Lindy had to hold out both arms in order to keep her balance.

"Sorry," she said, suddenly nervous even that far out. Her father had told her not to go in above her knees. The water was up to the bottom of her shorts. "I really can't."

"But—" Sealily began.

Coral shushed her. "It's okay, Lindy," she said. "Here—take the sponges. Maybe you'll want to try later."

"Um, okay." The sea sponges felt squishy and slimy in her hand. Lindy quickly stuck them in her pocket. "Thanks."

"If you want to visit us, swim straight

out to the east," Sealily began eagerly. "Then after you cross the big current . . ."

Lindy didn't bother listening to the rest of her directions. If she was too chicken to go with the mermaids now, no way would she have the guts to try it on her own! But she didn't want to hurt their feelings by saying so.

Finally Coral tugged on her sister's arm. "We should go. We can't let any other Drylanders see us."

"Are you sure you can't stay longer?" Lindy said.

"It's not safe for us," Coral said. "Maybe we'll come back another time."

She sounded doubtful, though. Lindy's heart sank as she realized she might never see the mermaids again. It didn't seem fair. She'd just met them!

"See you later, Lindy Drylander! Come

visit us soon!" Sealily waved, then dove into an oncoming wave.

Finneus let out a chirp and chased after Sealily. Coral smiled shyly. "Good-bye, Lindy."

"Good-bye, Coral."

Lindy watched, shading her eyes against the sun glinting off the water, until they were gone.

The Trade

Lindy sat on the beach for a while after the mermaids left, hoping they might come back. But they didn't, and finally her grumbling stomach reminded her that it was lunchtime.

Heading into the bug house, Lindy changed into dry shorts. She left on her swimsuit and the Cubs T-shirt, even though the shirt was damp. She was extra careful not to get any mustard on it as she made herself a sandwich.

By the time she finished eating, the shirt

was dry. She knew she should take it off—she was lucky she hadn't ruined it, wading into the ocean like that.

But it reminded her of her old home, her old best friend, her old life. Now that the mersisters were gone, that seemed more important than ever.

She went upstairs and looked at the sea sponges Coral had given her. They were on her dresser, where she'd set them when she'd changed her shorts. While she was eating, they'd dried into hard little lumps.

"Yuck," she whispered. She almost swept them into her trash can.

But even though they were kind of gross-looking, they were the only thing she had to remind her of her new friends. Just like her Cubs shirt was the only thing she had to remind her of Tara. Picking up the sponges, she stuck them in her pocket.

She wandered back outside. Her heart jumped as she saw movement by the old-man rocks. It wasn't the mermaids, though. Just Matthew poking around in the tide pool.

"Hey, New Girl!" he called, squinting up the hill at her. "Check out what I just found!"

He splashed out of the pool clutching a plastic bucket, the kind little kids used to build sand castles. Lindy wondered if he'd stolen it from his baby sisters.

"Awesome shirt," he said when he got closer. "Where'd you get it?"

Lindy glanced down at her Cubs T-shirt. "Where do you think? I'm from Chicago, remember?"

"Oh yeah." He shrugged. "I guess you're a baseball freak like me, huh?"

"No way," Lindy said quickly. She was

sure she didn't have *anything* in common with Matthew. "I don't care about sports."

He gave her a funny look. "So why are you wearing a Cubs shirt?"

"My best friend gave it to me." Lindy played with the hem of the shirt and thought about Tara. "It was a going-away present."

"Okay. Anyway, you'll never believe what I just caught. Look—it's a real sea horse!"

Matthew shoved the bucket at her. It smelled like rotten fish, and Lindy almost jumped away without looking. She didn't want him spilling his stinky, fishy water on her shirt.

Then she saw a small yellow shape inside. A *familiar* shape.

Finneus!

"Cool, huh?" Matthew bragged. "It's going to look awesome in my tank at home."

Lindy bit her lip. Finneus was cringing in the cloudy water at the bottom of the bucket. His dorsal fin was flat against his back.

Matthew looked in at the sea horse. "Hey, you!" he said loudly. He tapped on the side of the bucket. "Come on, swim around!"

"M-maybe you should let him go," Lindy said.

"Let him go? Are you crazy?" Matthew stared at her. "No way! I bet I'm the only person around here with a pet sea horse."

The only person above *the sea,* Lindy thought. She knew Coral and Sealily must be worried about their pet. How had the shy little sea horse ended up in Matthew's bucket?

Matthew tapped on the bucket again. "Stop that," Lindy said. "You're scaring him."

"Make me." Matthew tapped harder.

Lindy felt like crying. Poor Finneus! He would be miserable stuck in a tank with loud, annoying Matthew taking care of him.

He might not even survive! She had to think fast.

"You caught him on my family's property, right?" she said. "That means he's really mine, not yours. And I think you should let him go."

Matthew rolled his eyes. "Make me," he said again. Then he grinned. "Wait, I have an idea. If you like this sea horse so much, I'll trade him to you—for that shirt." He pointed to Lindy's Cubs T-shirt.

Lindy stepped back and tugged at her hair. "No way," she said. "Um, but I'll trade you something else. How about my allowance for next week?"

Matthew shrugged. "Uh-uh. It's the shirt or nothing." He turned and walked toward his own house.

"Wait!" Lindy said, feeling desperate. She

couldn't let him take Finneus home!

"What?" Matthew stopped and looked at her.

Lindy hesitated, touching her shirt. She thought about Tara, and Chicago, and her old life. Then she thought about Coral and Sealily. And Finneus.

"It's a deal," she blurted out.

"Huh?"

Lindy pulled the T-shirt off over her head. "Here," she said. "I'll trade."

8

Another Rescue

Matthew looked surprised. Then he grabbed the T-shirt out of Lindy's hand. "No backs-ies," he said.

He hurried toward the tide pool. "What are you doing?" Lindy asked.

"What does it look like?" He dumped the bucket into the shallow water. "I traded you the sea horse, not my bucket. You'll have to catch it again yourself."

With one last smirk, he raced away.

When Lindy peered into the tide pool, Finneus was huddled beneath a rock. "It's okay, Finny," Lindy said softly. "He's gone."

It took a few minutes to coax him out. At last the sea horse seemed to recognize her. He swam over and bumped her fingers with his head.

Lindy smiled. "You're safe now. Let's get you home."

She scooped him up carefully. Then she scrambled up the hill and down to the beach. Kicking off her sandals, she waded into the surf.

But releasing Finneus wasn't as easy as she'd expected. He was very small, and the waves tossed him back to shore as soon as Lindy let go of him.

"Sorry, Finneus!" she cried as he landed on the beach, flopping around and gasping for breath. She scooped him up and tried again, wading out farther this time. And even farther the time after that. Every time, Finneus ended up back on the beach.

Finally Lindy put him back in the tide pool. The little sea horse seemed relieved to be away from the rough waves.

"Now what?" Lindy whispered as she watched him swim around.

She wondered if she should carry him over to the cove, where the water was calmer. But she didn't have a bucket, and she didn't trust Matthew not to come back and capture Finneus again while she looked for one.

Besides, Matthew's house was on the cove. What if he spotted the sea horse over there? Or what if Finneus couldn't find his way out of the cove to the ocean?

Lindy felt like crying. "I need to get you out to deeper water," she told Finneus. "But how?"

Suddenly she had an idea. She raced to the house and grabbed a life jacket. Slipping it on, she fastened the buckles tightly.

There. Now she wouldn't have to swim. If the water got too deep or a wave knocked her over, she would float.

Lindy was shaking as she waded into the surf again, holding Finneus. But she knew what she had to do. She had to get out past the breaking waves. Then Finny could swim away without being tossed back to the beach.

Soon the water was up to Lindy's knees, then her thighs. She realized she'd forgotten to take off her shorts. She didn't want to turn around now, though. If she did, she might be too scared to try again.

"Almost there," she chanted. "Almost there."

Finneus wriggled in her hands, but she held on to him. They weren't quite deep enough yet.

Just ahead, she saw the spot where the waves started to swell up and get pushy. All she had to do was get past it. Then she could release Finny and go back.

She took another step. The waves splashed up past her waist. Almost there . . .

"Whoa!" she cried as her foot stepped forward—into nothingness!

She dropped Finneus and swung her arms, trying to push herself back onto the edge of the drop-off. But the push and pull of the waves dragged her. Her other foot lost its grip on the sandy seafloor. Just like that, Lindy was floating!

There was a happy chirp nearby. Finneus popped to the surface. He darted over and bumped her with his head.

"You're welcome," Lindy said breathlessly, realizing that she'd done it. The rough, breaking waves were behind them.

Way behind them. Lindy glanced back and gulped. The shore looked very far away.

Finneus chirped again. A second later he

disappeared beneath the surface, leaving Lindy all alone. The life jacket made it easy to float. But she still felt nervous.

"Better get back," she muttered. She pushed at the water with her arms to turn herself around. Then she kicked with both feet.

Yet the shore didn't get any closer. In fact, it looked even farther away! Lindy kicked harder, but it was no use.

She was caught in a riptide that was carrying her out to sea!

9

Lost at Sea

"Help!" Lindy cried. Her voice sounded weak and shaky. She thrashed her arms and legs. "Someone, please help!"

But the current was pulling Lindy farther from the island with every passing moment, and there was nobody in sight anyway. All she could think about was floating out to sea and being eaten by a shark. Her parents would never even know what had happened to her! Neither would Tara, or any of her other friends, or—

Suddenly Sealily's head popped into view!

Then Finneus appeared beside her.

"Lindy Drylander!" Sealily cried joyfully. "You came to see us!"

Coral surfaced beside her sister. "So that's what Finneus was so worked up about. Are you okay, Lindy?"

"Oh my gosh!" Lindy exclaimed. "I'm so glad to see you guys!" In a rush, she told them what had happened.

When she finished, Sealily shook her head. "Naughty Finny—he must have sneaked back to the Drylands to visit you!" she exclaimed.

"We thought so," Coral added. "That's why we came here to look for him. You saved him again, Lindy!"

"Yes, and now I'm the one who needs saving," Lindy said. "Can you help me get back to shore?"

"Of course. First we should pull you out of the current," Sealily said.

Coral looked dubious. "It's pretty strong here. It would be lots easier to get away from it by diving down."

"Down?" Lindy gulped. "Um, I don't think so."

"No, Coral's right, Lindy Drylander," Sealily urged. "If we dive down, we'll be out of the current in no time!"

Coral nodded. "Do you still have the sponges?"

For a second Lindy wasn't sure what she was talking about. Then she remembered.

"I have them," she said, fishing around for her shorts pocket. "But I thought you weren't sure if they'd work."

"We're not." Sealily giggled. "We're never sure about anything Thetis tells us."

Coral smiled at Lindy. "Just try, okay? We won't let you get hurt. Promise."

"Okay." Lindy was scared, but she couldn't help trusting Coral. As if they'd been friends forever.

She stuck one of the sea sponges into her left nostril. Ew! It felt weird and slimy in there. She almost yanked it right back out. Instead, she quickly shoved in the second sponge.

"Oh, this is so gross!" she exclaimed, breathing through her mouth. "It smells like old fish."

"Try to breathe," Sealily urged.

Lindy knew if she stopped to think much about it, she'd never do it. So she tipped forward, squeezing her eyes shut. Then she shoved her face into the water. As she did, she automatically gulped in a breath and almost snorted the sea sponges right up her nose!

"No, no!" Coral said as Lindy came up coughing and sputtering. "Close your mouth, then breathe the water in through only your nose."

"I'm not sure this is a good idea after all." Lindy wiped her face. "I can't even get my whole head under with this life jacket on."

"You need to take it off, Lindy Drylander," Sealily said. "We'll help you float."

Lindy gulped. "T-take off the life jacket?" Her heart pounded. But once again, she decided to try. If the breathing sponges didn't work, the mermaids could hold her up long enough to get the jacket back on. "Get ready to catch me if I sink," she said.

She wriggled out of the life jacket. Watching it float beside her made Lindy feel very small and helpless out there in the middle of the sea.

"Ready?" Coral hung on to Lindy's arm, helping her tread water.

Lindy was too nervous to speak. So she just nodded.

Then she sucked in a deep breath through her mouth . . . and let herself sink under the water. At first she kept her eyes shut. Then

she remembered to open them.

Coral was floating beside her, gazing curiously into her face. Her coppery hair swirled up around her head like a cloud. When Lindy turned her head, she saw that Sealily and Finneus were underwater, too.

"Don't hold your breath, Lindy," Coral said. Her voice sounded a little bubbly, but Lindy could hear her just fine. "Try to breathe. If you can't, we'll bring you right back to the surface."

Lindy nodded, still holding her breath. She felt something swish across her foot and gasped. Was it a shark?

She looked down and saw an eel swimming by. Whew! As it swam away, Lindy realized something.

"I'm doing it!" she cried. "I'm breathing underwater!"

10

Fins Forever

Sealily laughed with delight and did a flip. Finneus chirped excitedly.

"I knew it would work!" Coral cried.

"Come on." Sealily tugged on Lindy's hand. "We need to go deeper."

Lindy felt another little shiver of fear. She looked up and saw the surface shimmering a few feet over her head. The sun looked watery and pale through the sea.

Then she looked down. A pretty striped fish swam past, heading deeper. What other interesting things might be down there?

She squeezed Sealily's hand. "Okay. Let's go."

"Hold on," Coral said, grabbing Lindy's other hand. She and Sealily swooshed downward, with Finneus leading the way.

Lindy held on and kicked with her legs. Soon she felt the current let go of her. Still, they kept diving down, down, down. . . .

Finally they stopped. It wasn't as bright

down there. But once she got used to it, Lindy had no trouble seeing.

A whole new world lay before her. The pale sunlight picked up the colors of the sand and coral on the seafloor. Patches of bright green kelp swayed with the current like tall grass in a gentle breeze.

Fish were everywhere. Big fish, little fish, striped ones, plain ones. Big, flat ones

with googly eyes that stared at her as they wriggled past. Smaller, mottled ones with graceful waving fins that looked like a lion's mane. Schools of minnows that zipped past like liquid mercury. Flat silver angelfish outlined in turquoise and bright yellow. Even a leatherback turtle with flippers like wings.

"This is amazing!" Lindy exclaimed.

"Isn't it?" Sealily did another flip. Her tail fins sent bubbles racing toward the surface.

"That looks like fun." Lindy grinned. "Let me try!"

She kicked her legs, trying to copy the flip. The first part went okay. She kicked forward and felt herself turning upside down. Then she looked to the side to see how far she'd gone. That made her dizzy. She ended up drifting sideways, almost bumping into a passing manta ray.

Sealily laughed. "Not bad for your first time, Lindy Drylander."

"Don't laugh," Coral scolded her sister. "I'm sure we couldn't do a flip in the air of the Drylands."

Lindy laughed, too. "Neither can I."

She tried another flip and made it almost all the way around before tipping sideways again. That made all three of them laugh. Even being clumsy wasn't so bad under the sea!

After that, Lindy could hardly keep track of everything she saw. She and the mer-sisters swam by a colorful coral reef and a grove filled with jellyfish. They explored a shadowy kelp forest and the remains of an old shipwreck.

At first Lindy's legs felt awkward and slow compared to the mermaids' graceful tails.

But her swimming quickly got better. Before long she almost felt like a mermaid herself!

"What should we do next?" Sealily asked after a while. "How about dolphin riding?"

"I don't think we have time today," Coral said. "Soon Mother and Father will be looking for us."

"Oops." Lindy realized she had no idea how much time had passed. "Mine too. If I'm not back when they get home, they'll probably think a shark got me."

Finneus was still following them around. At the word *shark,* he squeaked and darted behind Coral.

"Don't worry, you silly wahoo," Sealily scolded him playfully. "There's no shark around."

"We'd better get you home, Lindy." Coral sounded disappointed. "Don't worry, we'll show you more next time you visit."

"For sure!" Sealily added. "Starting with. dolphin riding. It's so much fun, you won't believe it!"

Lindy wished she didn't have to leave. At least she had a lot to look forward to.

"I'll come back soon," she told her new friends. "I promise."

"There you are, Lindy!"

Lindy was sitting on the beach near the bug house reading a book by the pink and gold light of the setting sun. She looked up and saw her father hurrying toward her.

"Hi, Daddy," she said. "How was your day at the boat dock?"

"Fantabulous!" He was sunburned and had several new scrapes and scratches on his arms and legs. But he looked happy.

He reached down and ruffled Lindy's hair. "We missed you, though. Think you'll come along tomorrow?"

Lindy looked out at the ocean. Nobody would ever guess there was a whole world below its peaceful surface.

But now she knew. And she hoped to see more of it—soon. Until then, maybe she would try to see more of her new world *out* of the sea. Maybe it wouldn't be as bad as she'd thought.

"Sure, Daddy," she said with a smile. "I'd love to."

About the Author

Catherine Hapka has never lived on an island by the sea (though she has visited some) and has never met a mermaid (though she would like to). She loves all animals (including sea horses) and lives on a small farm in Pennsylvania with horses, goats, chickens, and too many cats. A full-time writer, she has published numerous books for children and young adults.